BY JAKE MADDOX

RUNNING BACK DREAMS

ILLUSTRATED BY SEAN TIFFANY

text by Eric Stevens

STONE ARCH BOOKS
a capstone imprint

Impact Books are published by Stone Arch Books
A Capstone Imprint
151 Good Counsel Drive, P.O. Box 669
Mankato, Minnesota 56002
www.capstonepub.com

Printed in the United States of America in Stevens Point, Wisconsin.
032010
005741WZF10

Library of Congress Cataloging-in-Publication Data
Maddox, Jake.
Running back dreams / by Jake Maddox ; text by Eric Stevens ; illustrated by
Sean Tiffany.
p. cm. -- (Impact books: a Jake Maddox sports story)
ISBN 978-1-4342-1637-3 (library binding), 978-1-4342-2781-2 (paperback)
[1. Football--Fiction.] I. Stevens, Eric, 1974- II. Tiffany, Sean, ill. III. Title.
PZ7.M25643Rtm 2010
[Fic]--dc22 2010006454

Art Director: Kay Fraser
Graphic Designer: Hilary Wacholz
Production Specialist: Michelle Biedscheid

Photo Credits: ShutterStock/Mike Flippo (p. 2, 3, 4, 5)

TABLE OF CONTENTS

Team JAKE MADDOX
Running
for Noah
29
29
WILDCATS
29
NOAH

ANDREW, LOGAN, COACH FRENCH, NOAH, CARLOS

SUBSCRIBE AND NEVER MISS AN ISSUE!
SPORTS UPDATE
ALL FOOTBALL ISSUE!
STATS

CHAPTER 1

STATS GUY

While the Wildcats played against the Buccaneers in front of him, Noah Hart sat on the bench.

His sports magazine was folded open on his left thigh. Under his helmet, on the bench next to him, was his big book of stats.

Noah's eyes stayed on the magazine. He scanned quickly through the article on a college running back.

The writer thought a college player, Jack Tyler, was going to be a great NFL player. Lots of pro teams wanted to draft him as soon as he graduated, since he was so amazing.

Noah wasn't convinced.

"Look at this," Noah said to the player next to him, Adam Glick. He didn't look up from the article. While he talked, he picked up the pen on his notebook and scribbled down some figures.

"This article says Jack Tyler is going to be the next big running back," Noah went on. "But look at these stats from late last season."

Noah tapped the paper of his notebook, and Adam looked down at the page. "What about them?" Adam asked.

"Don't you see?" Noah said. He finally looked up from his article and gazed at Adam. "In late-season games against strong defense, he falls apart," Noah explained. "He'll never make it in the pros. There's no way."

Adam frowned. "You think you know better than this writer does?" he asked. "And all those pro scouts?"

"You can quote me," Noah replied. Then he went back to reading his article.

A few moments later, a shadow fell over the magazine. Noah frowned.

He was about to shout, "Hey, get out of my light!" when Eric Floyd, the first-string running back, came tumbling into him. Eric was followed by three linemen from the other team.

SUBSCRIBE AND NEVER MISS AN ISSUE!
WILDCATS

Noah's magazine and stats notebook went flying. He fell backward off the bench and tumbled into the first row of the bleachers. His head slammed into the muddy ground with a thud.

"Ugh," Noah said. He struggled to get up, but slipped in the mud and fell right on his face.

The crowds above him in the bleachers, all the cheerleaders, and everyone on his team roared with laughter. Noah rolled onto his back and looked up at them.

He was covered from head to toe in mud. Even the guys who had been in the game weren't as muddy as he was.

"Get up, Noah!" Coach French shouted. He came stomping over.

"Oh, man," Noah muttered.

"Where is your head?" the coach snapped. "When that play came close to the sideline, everyone else on the bench got out of the way."

"They did?" Noah said. He got to his feet and wiped the mud off his face.

The coach handed him a towel. "Even Adam got out of the way," Coach French said. "And he was right next to you!"

"Sorry, Coach," Noah said. He wiped his face and hands with the towel.

Adam strolled over, smiling. "I tried to warn you, Noah," Adam said. "I guess you didn't hear me shouting at you."

"I guess not," Noah admitted.

"And you probably don't remember me tugging at your sleeve?" Adam said with a smirk.

"No," Noah said, gritting his teeth, "I don't remember that either."

The coach shook his head slowly. He was obviously disappointed in Noah, and Adam wasn't helping the situation at all.

"Just go hit the showers," the coach said. "It looks like you won't be getting any game time today. We'll talk after the game."

CHAPTER 2

After the game, Noah headed into the coach's office. The Wildcats had won, and they were celebrating in the locker room, but Noah knew he didn't get to take part in the celebration.

"Noah, you have to keep your nose out of those magazines and that stat book of yours," the coach said. He closed the door behind Noah and then sat down at his big metal desk.

Noah sat across from him in a little plastic chair. His hair was still wet from the shower.

"You have to keep your eyes on the game," the coach went on.

"I'm sorry, Coach," Noah said. "The thing is, I just love football so much. Sometimes I get caught up in an article. Have you heard about Jack Tyler? See, everyone thinks —"

Coach French cut him off. "Yes, I've heard about him," the coach said. "But that really doesn't matter, not when we're in the middle of a game against the Bloomfield Buccaneers."

"But, Coach," Noah said. "I hardly ever play. What's the difference if I'm not always paying super-close attention?"

The coach shook his head. "Even on the bench you're an important part of the team," he said. "Did you see that handoff to Eric?"

"No," Noah said.

"Did you see the mistakes the line made?" the coach went on. "Did you see the misstep Carlos took after the snap?"

Noah shook his head. "No, Coach," he said. "I missed the whole play. Except when Eric dove on top of me. I saw that part."

"A player like you can be a great part of this team," Coach French said. "You've got a great head for the sport. If you had been paying attention during that play, your knowledge of football would have been helpful to Eric, Carlos, and the whole offensive line."

COACH
FRENCH

"Thanks, Coach. I guess I didn't see it like that," Noah said.

The coach grunted. "Just pay attention," he said. "You're not much help if your nose is always in a magazine. On paper, those stats are meaningless. It's on the field that they count."

"Got it, Coach," Noah said quietly.

CHAPTER 3

That night after dinner, Noah headed up to his room.

"Are you doing your homework up there?" Noah's dad called up the steps a couple of hours later.

It was almost eight, and Noah's school books sat unopened on his desk. Noah glanced at them, then back at the screen of his laptop.

"Um, yes, Dad," Noah called back. But he wasn't doing his homework. He was looking at the website for his fantasy football league.

With Noah's love of football stats, his team was having a great season. Suddenly his computer dinged.

It was an instant message from Adam. Noah and Adam had become good friends because they sat on the bench together for most of every game.

ADAMINATOR: Noah, you there?

NOAHPOTOMUS: Hey, Adam. Just looking at the fantasy football scores. Your team isn't doing so well.

ADAMINATOR: Yeah, yeah. Tell me about your meeting with the coach. Did he scream at you or what?

NOAHPOTOMUS: He was angry, but I'm not worried.

ADAMINATOR: You're not? Don't you remember last year? Coach French kicked those two eighth-graders off the team for leaving the field during a game.

NOAHPOTOMUS: They went to get hot dogs! I was reading about football.

There was a knock at Noah's door. "Just a minute, Dad," Noah called.

NOAHPOTOMUS: Hey, I have to go. But remember, I haven't played more than two minutes in one game all season. What difference does it make?

"Noah, open this door!" his dad said from the hall.

"Just a second, Dad!" Noah called.

NOAHPOTOMUS: Oh, one more thing. Did you see the fantasy football scores? My team is still undefeated!

ADAMINATOR: I'm not surprised. I'll see you tomorrow.

NOAHPOTOMUS: Bye.

Noah slammed his laptop closed. Then he opened all his schoolbooks and jumped up to open the door for his dad.

"Hi, Dad," he said. "What's up? I'm working hard in here. I was just finishing a math problem."

His dad looked around the room. "Yeah, I can see you're working hard," he said. He frowned, but then his face relaxed. "All right, kiddo," he said. "Let me know if you need any help. I'll be downstairs."

FAMOUS TOUCHDOWNS

"Check this out," Noah said to Adam as they walked to the field before practice started the next afternoon.

He held out a magazine that looked older than either of them. It was sealed inside a clear plastic bag, like the ones Adam's older brother used to store his comic collection.

"What are you showing me?" Adam asked.

"This is a special magazine about the 1967 NFL Championship between Dallas and Green Bay," Noah said. "It was one of the best and most famous games in the history of football!"

The two boys sat on the front row of the bleachers. Noah read through the magazine while they waited for the rest of the team.

"Look at this," Noah said. He pointed at a full-spread photo of a touchdown.

It looked like nearly every player from both teams was piled in a heap on the goal line. In the front of the photo, an official, wearing his striped black-and-white jersey, had both of his arms straight up, signaling a touchdown.

"What's that?" Adam asked.

The Ice Bowl is considered to be one of the best games of football ever played! This is mainly due to the intensity of the weather, the rivalry between the two teams, how important the game was, and the intense conclusion to the game.

"This is one of the most famous touchdowns in football history," Noah explained. "Not only did it win the game for Green Bay, it also —"

A whistle blew close to Noah's ear. He jumped and almost dropped his magazine.

"Ow!" he said, turning toward the sound of the whistle.

Coach French stood next to him, glaring down at Noah.

"Um, hi, Coach," Noah stammered. Then he looked around.

The rest of the team was already gathered on the field, waiting for practice to start. Noah hadn't even noticed that Adam wasn't sitting next to him anymore.

"Um, sorry," Noah said.

He slipped his magazine back into its plastic bag. "I got caught up in this story about the 1967 NFL Championship," Noah went on.

"Yeah, I noticed," Coach French said, raising an eyebrow.

"Green Bay ran a sneak to win the game, Coach," Noah said. He put the magazine down and got up to join the others. "Even the coach didn't think it would work. But it did."

"Yes, I remember reading about that game," the coach replied. He put a hand on Noah's shoulder and guided him toward the other players on the sideline.

"Maybe we could use a sneak in the game against the Eagles next week?" Noah said. He pulled on his helmet.

"Thanks for the tip, Noah," the coach said. "But let's just run the plays we actually know, huh?"

He patted Noah on the helmet. Then he blew his whistle again and started going over the plays for the game against the Eagles.

Noah knew every play his team ran — and most other teams ran — by heart. He didn't need to listen to the coach repeating them. Before too long, his mind was wandering.

Noah didn't even realize that his coach was noticing.

CHAPTER 5

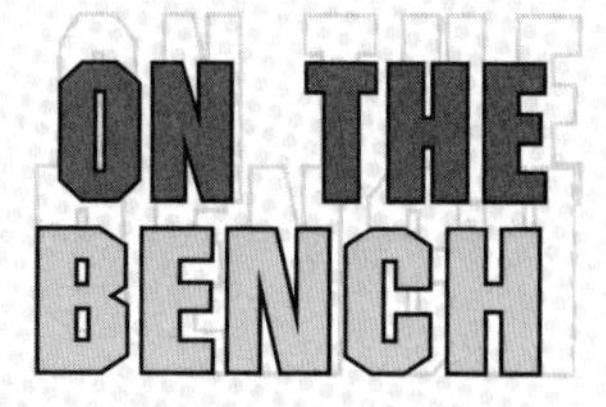

ON THE BENCH

The game against the Eagles was the following Thursday. Noah knew he wouldn't play much, if at all. He sat on the bench with his helmet between his feet. His stats notebook was on the bench next to him, between him and Adam.

"It's cold today," Adam said. He blew into his hands.

Noah nodded. "The news said it'll get down to freezing overnight," he said.

"I wish I were playing," Adam said. "Then I'd stay warm!"

Noah said, "There's no chance I'll play today. Coach is mad at me." He shrugged. "I don't know what to do about it. I can't just stop loving stats and football history."

He watched the game carefully, and noted every stat he could think of in his notebook.

"What are you writing down?" Adam asked.

"I'm keeping track of both teams' gains, what plays are working, tackles, sacks, completions . . ." Noah said. "You name it, I'm writing it down."

Adam shook his head. "Didn't Coach French tell you to keep your head out of your stats book?" he asked.

"I'm keeping stats on this game," Noah said. "That means not only do I get to record stats and go through my notebook, but I end up paying close attention to the team and the game, too. This should make everyone happy — me and the coach."

The boys both looked up at the field as their quarterback, Carlos Suarez, took a long snap. Carlos spun to his right, then cut left and handed off to Eric, the first-string running back.

Eric cut back to the right and then turned up field. He spun once to get through the defensive line, and then put his head down and started toward the end zone.

It was not a clear run, though. An Eagles defensive back was too fast even for Eric. He was on top of him in an instant.

WILDCATS

Eric tried to dodge, but he cut right into his blocker and they both went down. The Eagles back jumped on both of them and the whistle blew.

"Ow!" Eric screamed from the bottom of the pile-up. "My ankle!"

The whistle blew again as the Eagles defensive back and the Wildcats fullback got to their feet. The medics and Coach French ran out to the field.

Noah and Adam watched from the bench. It looked like Eric was really hurt. "That looks bad," Adam said quietly. Noah nodded. He was too shaken to even write down the stats of the play.

The coach and the medics crouched over Eric's ankle. Now and then, Noah could hear Eric yell out in pain.

After a few minutes, one of the medics ran to their truck. He came back carrying a stretcher.

"Oh no," Adam said. "Looks like Eric is coming out of the game."

Noah nodded. "I bet he sprained his ankle," he said. "I hope it doesn't ruin his whole season."

The fans and other Wildcats clapped for Eric as he was carried off the field.

Noah grabbed his pen and his stats book. He marked down the eight yards Eric had gained on the lead run, the play they'd just done. Then he marked that Eric had been injured and had to leave the game.

Noah looked up as Eric was loaded onto the stretcher. Coach French was heading in his direction, carrying Eric's helmet.

Noah looked back at his notebook and marked that the second-string running back would be entering the game.

Then he realized he was marking his own row in the stat book.

The second-string running back was him.

CHAPTER 6

YOU'RE IN

"You're in, Noah," Coach French said, patting him on the shoulder.

"Um, okay," Noah said nervously. "You got it, Coach."

Noah pulled on his helmet and jogged out to the huddle. He passed the two medics who were carrying Eric off the field.

Eric held up his hand as he went past. Noah gave him a high five. "Good luck," Eric said.

WILDCATS
80
29

"Thanks," Noah said. "I hope your ankle is okay."

Noah ran onto the field and joined the huddle. It was cold. His breath came out from his helmet like a puff of smoke. The whole huddle was full of clouds from the players breathing.

"Noah, we're going straight to you," Carlos said. Noah could see him smirking behind his facemask. "I hope you're feeling warmed up," Carlos went on. "Okay, on three, run counter."

Noah nodded. The play meant Carlos would try to get the defense off Noah with a fake. If it worked, Noah could run in open field.

If it didn't, Noah would be pretty much alone, with no blockers.

Carlos clapped and shouted, "Break!" The team got lined up in shotgun position.

Carlos barked at the center: "Hut, hut, hut!"

The center snapped the football. Carlos caught the ball and faded back to the left. The defensive line moved with him.

Noah ran to the left too, to take the handoff. As he ran, he spotted a defender on the Eagles line, number 66. He remembered number 66 from his stats book. Number 66 never fell for the fake.

Carlos turned and gave Noah the handoff as Noah cut back to the right side. The defense should have been weaker, but Noah glanced at the Eagles number 66. What if he wasn't fooled by the fake to the left?

Noah decided to cut back to the left, where the offensive line could protect him.

"Noah, weak side!" Carlos shouted, but it was too late.

Noah ran straight into the line, a mass of his own linemen and Eagles defensive linemen. The Wildcats linemen didn't expect Noah to come running up from behind them. They were confused and tried to make a path for him.

Instead they opened up and let the defenders rush through. They plowed into Noah, sending him flying deeper into the backfield and onto his back with a thud.

The whistle blew. Noah looked up at the sky. He watched his breath form a cloud over him for a second. It was bright white against the clear blue sky.

Carlos was standing over him. He reached out his hand to help Noah up, and Noah took it.

"Why'd you go left?" Carlos said.

Noah shook the tackle from his head and tried to reply. He heard the referee call out, "A loss of eight yards."

"There goes Eric's run," Carlos said. "And now it's third down." The quarterback shook his head and got into the huddle.

Noah followed him, hanging his head.

BLOWN IT

Carlos looked hard at Noah in the huddle. "We're running again, Noah," he said. "Power sweep. Wait for your guards, okay?"

Noah knew the play well. It would get some good yardage if the guards picked up the defenders in time. Otherwise, Noah would end up running straight out of bounds — or getting pounded into the grass again.

"Break!" Carlos shouted. The team lined up. Noah found his guards as the ball was snapped.

Both guards pulled right, and Noah fell in behind them. He knew he couldn't cut up field until the defense had been fully sealed off.

But the guards weren't big enough or strong enough to hold the defenders this time. The defensive line pushed through, and the hole wasn't big enough to slip through. Noah and his guards were being forced toward the sideline.

No way, Noah thought. *I'm not letting another loss of yards show up in my stats.*

Noah cut back to the left. The defenders were fooled for a moment, and Noah cut up the field.

It wasn't enough, though. The rest of the defensive line had already recovered and closed up the hole.

Noah threw up his arm and held the ball in one hand, like he'd seen so many great running backs do, but it didn't make any difference.

In an instant, he found himself face first in the grass. There was a clump of dirt and turf stuck in his facemask.

"Ugh . . ." he groaned. He just wanted to stay where he was.

The Eagles who had taken him down got up and high-fived. Noah managed to get to his feet too, but he wasn't feeling as good as they were.

The ref called out, "Loss of five yards. Fourth down."

Carlos walked past Noah and pulled off his helmet. "I guess we're not scoring this half," he said. "Here comes the kicking team."

Noah looked at the bench. Their kicker and special teams were heading for the field. Noah had blown it.

DO YOUR OWN THING

The Eagles scored a second field goal on their next and last drive of the half, making the score 6-0. Then, suddenly, it was halftime. Noah ran as fast as he could off the field and into the locker room, trying to stay warm.

Coach French led the halftime conference, going over plays and mistakes. With a couple of minutes left in halftime, he sent the boys back to the field.

Noah started walking out, but Coach French said, "Hold on a minute, Noah. I want to talk to you."

"What's up, Coach?" Noah asked. He tried to smile, but he knew the coach wanted to scold him for the mistakes he'd made in the first half.

"Noah, I don't know where your head is," the coach said. Noah looked down at the ground. "I thought you were just distracted when you were on the bench. You can't be looking at that stats book of yours while you're on the field."

"No, Coach," Noah said. "I'm not."

"Then what's wrong?" the coach asked, looking Noah in the eye. "You know those plays. Those are standard running plays — nothing fancy."

"Sure, I know them," Noah said. "I've run them a hundred times. And I've seen them run a thousand times or more."

"Then what happened out there?" the coach asked. "You went to the strong side on that first run, and on that second . . . well, you could have just run out of bounds and avoided getting plowed and the additional yard loss."

Noah took a deep breath. "The Eagles have a defender — number 66 — who never falls for a fake."

"Number 66?" the coach said. "That's Lawrence Crenshaw. He's a good player."

"Right," Noah said. "When I saw him on the line, I remembered his stats against fakes. I had a feeling he'd catch me on the weak side and clobber me."

"But he did fall for it," the coach said. "The right was wide open. You could have made a great gain, at least to the secondary."

"The stats said he'd catch me," Noah said. "I went with the stats."

The coach sighed. "Okay, what about that sweep?" he asked. "No stats there. Your guards didn't shut down the D. You should have run to the sideline, cut your losses."

"I was watching some old games over the weekend," Noah said. "I saw this great run by Earl Campbell —"

"Earl Campbell?" Coach French said. Then he held his stomach and laughed. "I'm sorry, Noah," he went on, still laughing. "But Earl Campbell might be the greatest running back of all time."

29
WILDCATS

"Exactly!" Noah said. "Shouldn't I learn from the best?"

The coach managed to stop laughing. He sat down next to Noah on the bench. "Sure," Coach French said. "Really, Noah, it's terrific that you follow the greats and know so much about the sport. Lots of guys on the team have no idea about the history of football."

"Well, I'm trying," Noah said.

"Earl Campbell could get through any line, Noah," the coach said. "He was like a truck. You're . . . well, sorry, kid, but you're just not."

Noah sighed. "I know," he said. "But I have to play to my strengths, right? And my strengths are knowing the great players and the great plays!"

"That doesn't mean you just try to be them," the coach replied. "It means you learn from them and try to apply those lessons to your own playing."

"What about stats?" Noah asked. "If I know number 66 on the Eagles is tough to fake, shouldn't I try something other than a fake?"

"Not necessarily," the coach said. "Maybe it just means you keep an eye on him during play-action or that you should let the team know that number 66 is a sneaky player."

"I guess," Noah said. "I think I'm starting to get what you're saying."

The coach got up and put a hand on Noah's shoulder. "Let's get back out there," he said.

"All right," Noah said.

"And remember," Coach French added, "sometimes it's a good idea to stick to what you know how to do. Forget what you know others have done. Do your own thing."

Coach French walked out of the locker room. Slowly, Noah stood up and followed him.

CHAPTER 9

SECOND HALF

The second half felt very long to Noah. Coach French and Carlos focused on the passing game. Though they made some good gains, Noah's only role was to pretend to take a handoff now and then for a play-action pass. Carlos called pass after pass.

Andrew Tucker made a few receptions, but it wasn't enough. As the end of the fourth quarter got closer, the Wildcats had only scored one field goal.

Their defense had been good, so the Eagles hadn't scored again. But that meant the score was still 6-3.

At the two-minute warning, it was third down. The Wildcats would need a field goal to tie and a touchdown to win.

"Just get us a few yards," Coach French said to Carlos. "We need to get into field goal range. Then we can win in overtime."

Carlos nodded as the official called for the teams to take the field again.

"They'll be expecting a run," the coach said. "So, Andrew, stop after about eight steps, and Carlos, just connect. Then our kicker will make the three."

The offense took the field. When they were lined up, Noah looked out over the defense.

Something wasn't right. The defensive line was stacked.

"Carlos," Noah said from the back. Carlos looked over his shoulder.

"They're rushing," Noah said. "They want to force us into fourth down with a loss and no options. Call blue 19."

"A toss sweep?" Carlos said. "That's crazy. They wouldn't risk taking their whole D out of the game. They know we can go long if they do. Besides, you can't outrun this defensive line."

"I won't have to," Noah said. "They'll only have two players who aren't on top of you by the time I start running!"

Carlos shook his head and started the count, but he glanced at the coach. Andrew started his jog across the backfield.

Noah stood up and called over to the sideline. "Coach!" Noah said.

Coach French looked at him, and Noah pointed to the defensive line, then at the cornerbacks. They looked ready to pounce.

The coach nodded, and then called out to Carlos. "Blue 19," Coach French said.

Carlos stopped the count and stood up straight. Then he stepped back into shotgun position and started the count again.

"Blue, 19," Carlos barked. "Blue, 19. Hut!"

The center snapped the ball and Noah cut hard to the left. Carlos immediately tossed the ball to Noah, just as the entire defensive line crushed through the Wildcats line. A moment later, they fell onto Carlos, but they were too late.

Noah had the ball. He ran as fast as he could up the sideline.

He easily got ten yards for the first down, and the end zone was in sight. Noah gave everything he had in every step. He could hear the breath and footsteps of the Eagles safety behind him.

The safety grunted and Noah felt arms wrap around his knees. His feet gave out just as he reached the goal line, but he held on to the ball and collapsed into the end zone.

Noah rolled onto his back in time to see the official throw up both his arms. "Touchdown!"

The rest of the offense came running up the field. Carlos pulled off his helmet as he ran.

WILDCATS
WILDCATS
16
WILDCATS

"That was amazing!" Carlos shouted.

"Great run!" Andrew said.

After a brief celebration in the end zone and the extra point kick, the score was 10-6, Wildcats. Noah clapped for the defense as they took the field. Coach French walked over to Noah.

"Great job, Noah," the coach said.

"Thanks, Coach," Noah replied.

"Do you know why that play went so well?" the coach asked.

Noah nodded. "Sure," he said. "I ran like Earl Campbell."

Coach French chuckled. "Really?" he said.

"No," Noah admitted. "But I played up my strengths."

Adam overheard the conversation and walked over. "What do you mean?" he asked.

"Well," Noah replied, "I saw how the defense lined up. I knew they would be trying anything to stop us from getting that first down."

"And you know that because of your expertise with stats, football history, and smart plays," Coach French added.

"And since I know all our plays so well," Noah said, "I was able to tell Carlos what a good play to call would be."

"You called that?" Adam asked. "I thought Carlos did!"

Noah laughed. "Before I got Coach French's attention," he said, "Carlos thought I was crazy!"

Carlos put his arm around Noah's shoulder. "Nah, I still think you're crazy," Carlos said, smiling. "But now I know it's worth it!"

THE AUTHOR

ERIC STEVENS

ERIC STEVENS LIVES IN ST. PAUL, MINNESOTA WITH HIS WIFE, DOG, AND SON. HE IS STUDYING TO BECOME A TEACHER. SOME OF HIS FAVORITE THINGS INCLUDE PIZZA AND VIDEO GAMES. SOME OF HIS LEAST FAVORITE THINGS INCLUDE OLIVES AND SHOVELING SNOW.

15

24

THE ILLUSTRATOR

SEAN TIFFANY

WHEN SEAN TIFFANY WAS GROWING UP, HE LIVED ON A SMALL ISLAND OFF THE COAST OF MAINE. EVERY DAY UNTIL HE GRADUATED FROM HIGH SCHOOL, HE HAD TO TAKE A BOAT TO GET TO SCHOOL! SEAN HAS A PET CACTUS NAMED JIM.

GLOSSARY

attention (uh-TEN-shuhn)—concentration and careful thought

convinced (kuhn-VINSSD)—made someone believe you

disappointed (diss-uh-POINT-id)—let someone down by failing to do what he or she expected

distracted (diss-TRAKT-id)—if you were distracted, you had your concentration weakened by something else

knowledge (NOL-ij)—the things that someone knows

meaningless (MEE-ning-less)—without meaning, having no importance

obviously (OB-vee-uhss-lee)—easily seen or understood

situation (sich-oo-AY-shuhn)—the circumstances that exist at a certain time

stats (STATS)—short for statistics, facts or pieces of information

DISCUSSION QUESTIONS

1. Noah is obsessed with football facts. What are some good things about that? What are some bad things?
2. How did Noah's love for stats get him in trouble?
3. If you were Noah's friend, what could you do to help him?

WRITING PROMPTS

1. Noah is on a team with his good friend Adam. Write about a friend with whom you share an interest. What do you do together?
2. Noah loves stats. Write about something you really love.
3. Pretend that you're a reporter. Write a newspaper article about the game against the Eagles.

MORE ABOUT RUNNING BACKS

In this book, Noah Hart is a running back for the Westfield Wildcats. Check out these quick facts about running backs.

- A running back's main jobs are to receive handoffs from the quarterback, to catch passes, and to block.
- The Heisman Trophy, given to the best college player each year, is topped with a small statue of a running back. It was modeled after Ed Smith, a running back who played for New York University, the Boston Redskins (in 1936), and the Green Bay Packers (in 1937).
- Famous running backs have included Brian Mitchell, Brian Westbrook, Steven Jackson, Larry Centers, Marshall Faulk, Jim Brown, Earl Campbell, Barry Sanders, and Reggie Bush.

81
WILDCATS
81
WILDCATS
16
16

THE WILDCATS

WAIT!
DON'T close the book!
There's MORE!
WILDCATS
54
FIND MORE:
Games
Puzzles
Heroes
Villains
Authors
Illustrators at...
www.
capstonekids
.com
Still want MORE?
Find cool websites and more books like this
one at www.Facthound.com.
Just type in the Book ID: 9781434216373
and you're ready to go!